This book belongs to

....

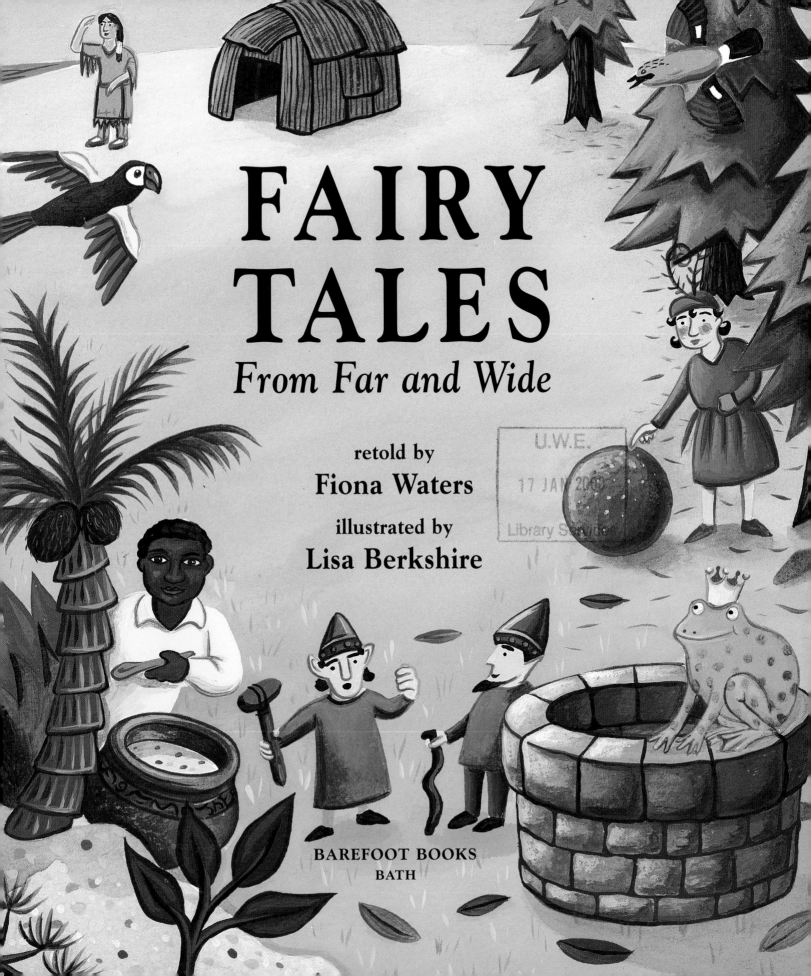

FAIRY
TALES

From Far and Wide

retold by
Fiona Waters

illustrated by
Lisa Berkshire

BAREFOOT BOOKS

BATH

Contents

The Frog Prince

German

Once upon a time, when magic still worked, there lived a rather spoilt princess. She had hundreds of beautiful dresses and even more pairs of shoes. She had rings on every finger and fine combs in her long golden hair. She ate off golden plates and drank from golden goblets. She slept in a huge bed with soft silky sheets and warm blankets.

One afternoon the princess took her most favourite play-thing, a golden ball, and wandered outside into the shady forest that surrounded the palace. She found herself by a well so she sat down and began to throw the golden ball high into the air, catching it again as it came down. Suddenly, a finger of sunlight pierced the leaves of the trees and dazzled the princess. Alas, the golden ball fell into the water with a heavy splash and sank deep into the darkness of the well.

The princess peered over the edge but she could see no sign of the treasured golden ball. She began to cry for she thought it was lost forever. Then she heard a croaky voice saying, 'Princess, princess, what is the matter?'

Startled, she looked around but could see no one. She cried even more bitterly, and again the voice came, 'Princess, princess, why are you crying?'

When she peered more closely she saw a very large frog sitting by the edge of the well.

'Gracious!' thought the princess. 'A talking frog!'

The frog hopped a little closer. The princess wrinkled her nose. The frog looked wet and slimy and he was rather close to her foot.

'If you must know,' she said crossly, 'my precious golden ball has fallen into the well.'

'Is that all?' said the frog. 'I can fetch it in the twinkling of an eye.'

'Dear frog, I will give you great riches if you bring my ball back to me,' said the princess.

'I don't want great riches,' said the frog. 'But if I fetch your ball, I would like in return to come and live with you in the palace and eat off your plate and sleep by your pillow.'

The princess thought that this was just nonsense but she did want her ball back. She dried her eyes and smiled weakly at the frog.

'Dear frog, you shall have whatever you want.'

No sooner were the words out of her mouth than there was a plop, a swirl of water, and the dripping frog stood by her foot once more, with the golden ball in his mouth. The princess was delighted! She snatched the ball and ran back towards the palace. She did not stop to say 'thank you' to the frog. She did not hear him calling, 'Princess, princess, wait for me.'

But as the princess sat down to supper that night with the king and queen, they heard a strange sound outside, like wet feet flapping on marble. Then there came a voice, 'Princess, princess, remember your promise by the well.' The door opened and in hopped the frog.

Now the king was a good man, and when the princess had told him what had happened at the well he said, 'My daughter, you made a promise. You must keep it.'

So the footman lifted the frog up and put him on the table beside the princess's plate. The frog ate delicately but the princess quite lost her appetite. Then the frog said, 'Thank you, princess. I should like to go to bed now.'

The princess winced but the king reminded her, 'My daughter, you made a promise. You must keep it.'

So she picked the frog up by one leg and carried him at arm's length to her bedroom. He hopped on to the pillow and went to sleep. The princess spent the night wide awake, at the other end of the bed.

The next evening, the frog was back and the princess had to share her supper and her pillow again. The third night, the same thing happened but this time the princess slept soundly. When she woke up the frog was gone, but standing by her bed was a handsome prince! He told the astonished princess that he had been bewitched by a wicked fairy and only if a real princess would let him share her plate for three days and her bed for three nights would the spell be broken.

Needless to say, there was great rejoicing when the prince told his story all over again to the king and queen, and while everyone was feeling so jolly he asked the princess to marry him. The princess put the golden ball in a safe place, and she did become rather less spoilt. And when she had children of her own, she taught them all to keep their promises.

The Sun Egg

Swedish

L ong, long ago there was a wee tiny elf living in the forests of Sweden. All the woodland creatures loved her for her gentle ways, especially the birds.

One day, as she was wandering through the woods, she found a large, round, brightly coloured something that looked rather like the birds' eggs she had often rescued from the forest floor.

'Whatever can this be?' she said. 'It looks like an egg but it is SO big.'

Just then a shaft of sunlight glanced through the trees.

'Oh! It must be a sun egg which has dropped down from the sky. Whatever shall I do?'

She ran off to see if she could find someone to help her decide what to do with the sun egg when suddenly something hit her on the head.

'Ouch! Now what is falling from the sky?'

But then she heard laughter and she realised it was her friend Larch, another elf who was always playing tricks. She looked up and there he was lying on a branch of a tree. He had thrown a fir cone at her.

'That hurt! Now I shan't tell you my secret,' she said as she ran off again.

Larch dropped down from the tree. He was sorry he had hurt her, and he did want to share the secret, so he ran off after her.

The elf had a very special friend called Happy Frog who had a little restaurant by the side of the lake. By the entrance to the restaurant was a sign saying 'Guests Are Forbidden To Eat Each Other', and usually her customers were very well-mannered. Anxious Frog and a snail were having their lunch when the elf ran up.

'Oh, do come and see,' said the elf. 'I have found a sun egg and I don't know what to do with it.'

Happy Frog and Anxious Frog hopped after the elf as she dashed back into the forest while the snail slid down off his seat. When they all caught up with each other, which in the snail's case wasn't until the middle of the next week, they found Larch already there with Squirrel.

'Do you think this means we can have our own sun shining here all the time once it hatches out?' asked the elf.

'I certainly hope not,' said Owl as he peered at the assembled company from high up in his tree. 'I couldn't go out at night if there wasn't any night, if you see what I mean.'

While the others were thinking about that, Larch walked round the egg.

'Do you think it has a fire in the centre?' he asked. 'The sun does, you know.'

'What is all this talk about fire?' asked a rather cross voice.

It was Crooked Root, the old gnome who was in charge of the forest.

'If there is a fire I must know about it, and it must be put out immediately,' he said loudly.

Happy Frog suggested rolling it into the lake where it could hatch out without setting fire to anything. Squirrel bit off a piece from the outside.

'Ugh! It tastes really bitter and nasty.'

'Oh, do be careful,' cried the elf, her voice rising above the hubbub as everyone talked at once. A thrush flew down by her side as he heard the distress in her voice.

'What is the matter?' he said looking at the anxious elf.

'I have found this sun egg and I am afraid the chick inside will be hurt if anyone touches it,' she said.

'Don't be upset, little friend,' said the thrush. 'This isn't a sun egg, it is an orange. It is a fruit that grows in a far-off hot land. I can't imagine how it came here. It is full of delicious sweet juice. Perhaps Happy Frog ought to have it in her restaurant.'

Well, as soon as he said 'full of juice', everyone started poking the orange with sharp sticks to get the juice out. They were making so much noise that a huge crow who happened to be passing stopped to take a look. As soon as he saw the orange, down he swooped and stole it from under their noses.

'My beautiful sun egg,' sobbed the elf. 'Now I shall never see one again.'

'Dry your tears, little friend,' said the thrush. 'I shall take you to the hot lands on my back when I fly back there this autumn. You are as light as thistledown, I shan't notice the extra weight.'

And so that autumn the little elf did fly to the hot lands on the back of the thrush and she saw hundreds of sun eggs and butterflies and huge, brightly coloured flowers and all kinds of wonderful things. But when the spring came she asked the thrush to take her back to Sweden to dance the snow away so that the wood anemones would poke their heads up in the forest again. But she never forgot her first beautiful sun egg.

Little Red Riding Hood

French

Here is a tale about a sneaky old wolf and a little girl who didn't remember what her mother had told her about not talking to strangers.

This little girl lived with her mother on the edge of a dark wood. Her granny had made her a warm cloak in bright red flannel with a great big hood and so everyone called her Little Red Riding Hood.

One day her mother asked her to go and visit her granny who lived in the middle of the dark wood.

'Little Red Riding Hood, Granny is not very well and I am sure it would cheer her to have a visit from you,' she said. 'I have made some soup for her and a nice pie.'

So Little Red Riding Hood put on her red cloak and took the basket down from the kitchen table.

'You must go straight to Granny without stopping. Keep to the path and whatever you do, don't talk to

any strangers. Do you promise me, now?' asked her mother.

'Yes, Mother. I promise,' said Little Red Riding Hood and off she set. It was a lovely day and all the wild flowers looked so pretty.

'Perhaps Granny would like some flowers to have by her bedside,' thought Little Red Riding Hood. Well, she kept on seeing better ones just beyond her reach, and before she really knew it, she was in a part of the wood she had not seen before. She suddenly remembered her promise to her mother and turned round to go back. But then WHAT a fright she had for there, standing in the middle of the path, was the most enormous wolf!

She gave a big scream, but the wolf just smiled at her.

'Hello, little girl. And where are you going to with that lovely bunch of flowers?'

The wolf smiled so nicely and looked so friendly and spoke so gently that Little Red Riding Hood completely forgot her promise not to talk to strangers.

'Hello, Mr Wolf. I am going to visit my granny who is not feeling very well today.'

'Oh, I am sorry to hear that,' said the wolf, who was not in the slightest bit sorry. He was just thinking how tasty the little girl would be and perhaps the granny was at least another mouthful. He decided to run on ahead to her granny's cottage.

'I must dash now,' he said. 'I do hope you find your granny in better shape.'

'In better shape in my tummy,' he sniggered to himself as he loped off down the path. He soon found the cottage and, peering in through the window, he saw Little Red Riding Hood's granny lying there in bed. Quick as a flash he opened the door and gobbled her up. Then he put on her night cap and arranged himself in bed. He heard Little Red Riding Hood tap at the door.

'Hello, Granny. It is Little Red Riding Hood. Please may I come in?'

'Of course, my dear,' said the wolf in as creaky an old voice as he could manage. 'Come in, come in.'

Little Red Riding Hood came in and held out her bunch of flowers.

'I picked these for you on my way here, Granny.'

The wolf held out a paw and grabbed the flowers.

'Why, Granny, what great big hands you have.'

'All the better to hug you with,' said the wolf, peering over the bedclothes.

'Why, Granny, what great big eyes you have.'

'All the better to see you with,' said the wolf, with a nice smile.

'Why, Granny, what great big teeth you have.'

'All the better to eat you with,' said the wolf, leaping out of the bed.

And in one great gulp, he swallowed up Little Red Riding Hood.

He felt very tired with his huge tummy full of Granny and Little Red Riding Hood, so he lay down on the bed and was soon fast asleep. But he slept so heavily that he began to snore. He snored louder and louder and the plates began to rattle on the table. He snored even louder and the windows began to shake.

Now a huntsman was passing by and he heard the terrible snoring. He knew Little Red Riding Hood's granny lived there alone and he just couldn't believe she was making such a noise. He peered in through one of the windows and there was the wolf, still fast asleep. 'Right, Mr Wolf! I have been after you for a very long time. I bet you have swallowed the old lady whole, you greedy thing.'

The huntsman tiptoed into the bedroom and with granny's scissors he cut a great slit in the wolf's fat tummy. Out popped Granny and, to his great surprise, out popped Little Red Riding Hood too! Before the wolf could wake up, Little Red Riding Hood filled his tummy with stones and sewed up the slit. With a snarl, the wolf awoke and tried to stand up, but he was so heavy that he dropped down dead. Well, you can imagine the rejoicing as everyone sat down for a good cup of tea.

Little Red Riding Hood was always rather wary of wolves after that.

The Black Bowl

Japanese

Along time ago in ancient Japan there lived an elderly couple who had one daughter. She worked all day beside her father in the rice fields and in the evening she turned her hand to cooking their meal, fetching the water and cleaning the house. She wore only a simple homespun dress and always went barefoot, but she never complained and had the sweetest nature.

Now one sad day her father died and her mother called the daughter to her bedside.

'My daughter, it will not be long before I join your father so you must listen to me carefully.' The poor girl could not stop crying.

'My daughter, do you know that you are very beautiful?' asked the mother.

'Am I?' asked the daughter, for she had never seen herself in a mirror.

'And my daughter, do you know that you have very fine manners?' asked the mother.

'Do I?' asked the daughter, for she had never visited other people.

'My daughter, you must do just as I say otherwise it will go badly for you. Bring me our black rice bowl from the stove,' said the mother. The girl did as she was asked. Imagine her astonishment when her mother placed the bowl over her head!

'You must never remove this bowl from your head, my daughter. Promise me this.' The girl promised faithfully that the bowl would remain on her head always. Not long after this, the old lady died and the poor girl was left all alone in the world. She planted flowers on her parents' grave and set off to seek her fortune.

She really was a very odd sight with the great black bowl on her head and everywhere she went she was greeted with mockery and insults. No one noticed her quiet voice or her gentle manners. Children would throw stones at her and she was driven out of many a village as if she were a demon.

One day she was sitting by a stream cooling her dusty feet when a rich farmer's wife came by. When she saw the poor girl sitting by the river, she stopped and spoke to her. 'Who are you, and why do you sit by the river with that great black bowl on your head?'

The girl said quietly that she was seeking work. The farmer's wife was impressed with the girl's good manners and, if the truth be told, she was greatly intrigued by the bowl.

'If you walk a little way down this road, you will come to my husband's farm. We will give you work.'

The farmer's wife was true to her word and the grateful girl worked hard in exchange for food and a roof over her head. But she would never answer any questions about the great black bowl.

One day the farmer's wife came to the girl, bursting with excitement. 'My son who lives in

Kyoto is coming home to visit us! I would like you to help me with the preparations. But when he arrives, you must keep well hidden, for I can't imagine what he would think about you and that great black bowl.' The young girl understood well enough that she would be an embarrassment to the couple who had been kind to her so, when the son arrived at the farm with his smart friends, she hid herself in the wine cellar.

The celebrations went on and on. The shouts of laughter reached the girl but she never moved from her hiding place.

Presently she heard footsteps coming down to the wine cellar, and there standing in front of her was none other than the son! She was greatly frightened and he was greatly puzzled. Who was this girl with a huge black bowl on her head?

After this, the son forgot all about going back to Kyoto. Instead, every day he made it his business to seek out the girl. He talked to her and tried to peek under the great black bowl. It wasn't too long before he told his parents that he intended to marry her, great black bowl and all. Well, you can imagine the fuss! His mother wept and wailed, his father shouted and stormed, but the young man had made up his mind.

The wedding day dawned. All the young girls in the village came to dress the bride. They arrayed her in rich brocades and costly silks. 'Now come, off with this great ugly black bowl and let us put gold combs in your hair,' they cried, but no matter how much they tugged, the bowl would not come off. The bride-to-be never said a word as they led her to the bridegroom.

Rice wine was poured from a silver flagon into a silver cup and the couple drank from it together as they were pronounced man and wife. Then, with a great loud crack, the black bowl burst asunder and a shower of glittering gold coins fell to the ground, a dowry fit for a princess. But the bridegroom had eyes only for his beautiful wife who stood before him, smiling like the sun.

As for the pieces of the great black bowl, the farmer's wife lost no time in throwing them on to the fire!

The Smith and the Little People

Irish

Now this is a tale of the Little People and their tricks. Far to the west of Ireland lie some wild scattered islands, lapped by the Atlantic Ocean. Here there once lived a blacksmith and his only son. The son was a big strapping lad, and the apple of his father's eye. They lived a simple contented life, well respected by their few neighbours.

One day the father rose early as usual and was puzzled to find his son still a-bed.

'Come, son, it is time to get up!'

But the boy just lay there saying nothing.

'Now then, my son. We have work to do!'

But the boy still just lay there, saying nothing.

The father fetched a light and was shocked to see his fine young son looking white and thin and suddenly strangely old. All day he

just lay there, saying never a word. The next day was the same and the next and the next. The father couldn't work for anxiety and he too just sat all day, watching his son slowly fading away. It was a desperate state of affairs. And then, by great good fortune, a travelling Wise Man happened to pass by.

He took one look at the boy and said to the blacksmith, 'Hah, you will never get this lazy lump out of bed! This isn't your son, it is a changeling, left here by the Little People. They have stolen your son!'

The blacksmith was distraught. 'Tell me, how can I get my beloved son back?'

'I will help you get your son back but it will not be easy. The Little People do not let their captives go readily.'

The Wise Man took the blacksmith outside and pointed to the Green Knowle, a huge green hill that had stood outside the village for as long as anyone could remember.

'Your son will be inside the Green Knowle.'

Well, the poor blacksmith just collapsed, and began to wail, 'I will never see my beloved son again. Oh dear, what shall I do?'

'Well, you can stop all that nonsense for a start,' said the Wise Man rather sharply. 'First you must light a fire in the bedroom, and when the fire is really blazing, pick up the changeling and fling it into the depths of the fire. Do you have the courage?'

The blacksmith dashed away his tears.

'I will do anything to get my son back again.' So he built a huge fire in the bedroom, watched all the time by the thing in his son's bed. Its eyes became fearful as the flames leapt higher and suddenly the blacksmith heard a thin little voice saying, 'What are you doing?'

'THIS is what I am doing,' said the blacksmith and he picked up the changeling and flung it into the depths of the fire. There was a terrible shriek, and a huge hole appeared in the roof. Of the changeling there was not a sign.

'Well done,' said the Wise Man rubbing his hands together. 'Now comes the really difficult part. At the next full moon you must enter the Green Knowle. Take a Bible, a sword and a cockerel hidden under your cloak. As soon as you see your son, grab him and run for your lives. The Little People will try to hold fast to you both but if you release the cockerel, they will be confused into thinking it is dawn when they must be back underground and you should be able to make good your escape.'

So the next full moon the blacksmith was to be found shaking outside the Green Knowle. And sure enough a door slowly slid open at the foot of the hillside. The blacksmith took a deep breath, propped the door open with his sword and strode in. He was momentarily dazzled for there inside a brightly lit chamber were hundreds and hundreds of the Little People but, most joyous to him, there was his poor son, with a slow smile dawning across his face as he recognised his father.

A great yell of rage rose from the Little People as they realised there was an intruder in their hall. The blacksmith held up his Bible high in the air and the yell dropped to a hiss as the Little People fell back from him. The son stretched out his hand and together they ran towards the door. There rose a great muttering as the Little People tried to trip and hinder the two. The blacksmith released the cockerel, crowing lustily, and in the confusion they rolled through the door on to the grass outside. The sword came flying through the air after them and the door slammed shut.

Great was the happiness in the village when the two came back and the celebrations lasted for many days. The blacksmith and his son grew rich and prosperous. It was often said by strangers laughingly that any sword forged by the son was so fine and remarkable that he might have been taught by fairy blacksmiths. The son just smiled.

Strong Wind the Invisible

Native American

By the shores of the wide, grey Atlantic Ocean there once lived a great warrior. He was a wise and courageous man but he also had a strange power which enabled him to do many amazing things. He could even make himself completely invisible. His name was Strong Wind the Invisible.

Strong Wind lived with his sister but many young maidens were keen to marry him. He had let it be known that he would only marry the girl who could see him coming home in the evening. Many had tried but all had failed. Only his sister could see him as he walked along the shore. When they were tested, the girls who wanted to marry him would lie saying, 'Oh yes, I can see him! He is coming out of his boat.' But when his sister asked, 'And what has he in his

hand?' no one could give the right answer. Each time, Strong Wind's sister knew that the girl was lying. She told her brother that he could not marry a woman who was not truthful.

Now in the same village there lived a great chief who had three daughters. Their mother had been dead for a very long time. The youngest daughter was gentle and loving but her older sisters were mean-spirited, selfish and very jealous of their sister who was as beautiful as her heart was warm. One night, they cut off her long hair that was as black as the raven's wing, they daubed her face that was pale and fair as the moon with ashes from the fire and they dressed her in rags. Despite this, the youngest daughter said nothing and went about her daily work with patience and a smile for everyone.

The chief's two oldest daughters, of course, thought they were most suitable partners for Strong Wind and tried to win his hand. But their lies were soon found out and Strong Wind remained with his sister in their tent by the shores of the wide, grey Atlantic Ocean.

One day, the youngest daughter decided that she would like to live away from her unkind sisters and thought she would try her luck with Strong Wind. So, without much success, she tried to wash her face, comb her hair and patch her tattered clothes. When her cruel sisters heard what she was going to do, they laughed at her scornfully, saying, 'How can you imagine an old tattercoats like you could possibly succeed where we have failed?' But the youngest daughter said nothing and walked down to the shore with a gentle smile on her face.

Strong Wind's sister welcomed her warmly, for she had heard only good things about the chief's youngest daughter. She did not comment on her shabby appearance. They walked along the beach together and presently Strong Wind's sister said, 'Do you see where Strong Wind approaches?' But the girl answered, 'No.' Again she asked, 'Do you see where my brother walks?' And again the girl answered, 'No.' Strong Wind's sister was very surprised as no one had ever answered truthfully before. A third time she asked, 'Strong Wind is close to us. Can you see him?' This time the chief's daughter answered in a voice of great wonder, 'Oh yes, I can see him now! He is drawing his sledge.' Strong Wind's sister asked quietly, 'And what is he pulling his sledge with?'

The girl answered in amazement, 'He is pulling his sledge with the rainbow.' Then Strong Wind's sister understood that her brother

must have made himself visible to the girl, but she asked one final question, 'What is my brother's bow-string?' The chief's daughter answered unhesitatingly, 'His bow-string is the glorious Milky Way.' Laughing, Strong Wind's sister wrapped her arms round the girl. 'Now I know my brother has truly found a woman worthy of him!' Then she took the chief's daughter to their tent by the shores of the wide, grey Atlantic Ocean and she washed away all the ash and grime from her beautiful face, so that it shone once more, pale and fair as the moon. She combed her dark hair, black as the raven's wing, and it grew long and silky again. She gave the girl rich, warm clothes to wear and many fine necklaces and set her in her own place beside Strong Wind.

The very next day, Strong Wind made the chief's youngest daughter his wife and they lived together happily ever after. They were famous far and wide for their great deeds, their wisdom and the warmth of their welcome to passing travellers.

And what of the two older sisters? Strong Wind resolved to punish them forever. He turned them both into aspen trees and to this day, the leaves of the aspen always tremble in fear at the coming of the wind, for they can never forget Strong Wind's great anger at their cruelty to his gentle wife.

Anansi and the Magic Pot

West Indian

This is a story of how Anansi the trickster was tricked. One morning Anansi was wandering through the forest towards the river when suddenly he almost fell over a pot lying on the path in front of him. It was a large round pot, smooth on the inside and with strange letters carved round the outside. 'I wish I knew what the letters round the edge mean,' he said out loud to no one in particular.

'Fill the pot,' said a quiet voice beside him.

'Who said that?' asked Anansi.

'Fill the pot,' said the quiet voice again and this time Anansi could have sworn it was the pot that had spoken.

'Fill the pot?' he repeated in his astonishment and before he had time to collect his scattered wits, the pot was filled to the brim with the most delicious-smelling chicken stew.

Being a greedy man, he promptly sat down and gobbled the whole lot up, without pausing for breath or to think where the food might have come from or, indeed, to whom it might belong.

'That was a splendid feast. When can I have another one?' he said without so much as a 'by your leave' or a 'thank you' to the pot. But the pot replied quietly, 'Just repeat the words, "Fill the pot" and you will have whatever you ask for. But you must never ever wash me out or my magic powers will cease.'

Well, Anansi was so selfish he didn't even think about sharing his wonderful discovery with his wife or his children. He hid the pot under some bushes and went home as if nothing unusual had happened.

The very next day, he rushed to the hiding place. 'Fill the pot,' he demanded and immediately it was filled to the brim with the most delicious roast pork and red beans. He polished off the lot, and again didn't think of sharing his good fortune with anyone else.

And so it went on for several days. Anansi would come out and command the pot to produce whatever he desired, eat it, and then return to his poor, hungry family. Before too long, however, his family became suspicious.

'How come Papa eats the same as us and yet he gets fatter and fatter?' asked his eldest son.

'Hush your mouth, child. Don't you go talking about your Papa like that,' said Anansi's wife, but secretly she thought her husband must be up to his old tricks and so she watched him carefully.

One morning she followed him through the forest some way behind, and she saw him lift the pot out from its hiding place and then sit down to a huge helping of delicious-smelling vegetable stew.

My, she was cross! But she went home quickly and served up the family's usual frugal meal without saying anything about her discovery. The next morning, however, she rose very early while Anansi was still asleep, and went herself to the hiding place. She took the magic pot from under the trees and had a very close look at it.

'What has my tricksy husband been up to? This is a very beautiful pot, even though it is so dirty. Perhaps if I wash it, someone will buy it from me and we can all have some good food to eat!' So she took the magical pot, not realising that it was magic, down to the river and gave it a good scour out.

When Anansi woke, he was not surprised to find his wife missing. She usually rose long before him because she had so much work to do. And in any case, he was too busy deciding what he would ask the pot for that day. You can imagine his dismay when he found the pot was not in its usual hiding place. He looked everywhere but the pot had vanished. He eventually gave up his search and went back home, feeling very disgruntled and very hungry.

He was astonished to find his wife cooking a huge meal with all kinds of delicacies such as their poor house had not seen for many a long day. 'Wife, where did you get all this wonderful food?' he asked.

'Well, husband, I had the most strange dream last night. I dreamt I found this beautiful pot filled with food hidden in the forest not far from here and when I awoke this morning I went and looked for it. And do you know, husband, there it was. Is that not amazing?'

'Yes, yes, amazing,' said Anansi desperately. 'But what did you do then?'

'I washed it out very carefully and took it to market where I sold it for a great deal of money. Are you not pleased with me, husband? We will have enough food for many a long day,' she said proudly, but with a glint in her eye too.

Of course Anansi couldn't say anything without giving himself away, so he just went and sat in the forest for a very long time until he had recovered his temper. For once, Anansi the trickster had been tricked himself!

Sources for the Stories

The Frog Prince
This tale was first recorded by the Brothers Grimm but was known long before then. They called it one of the oldest tales in Germany but variants of the theme are to be found in many cultures.

The Sun Egg
Elsa Beskow was born in Sweden in 1874. After attending art school, she married and had six sons for whom she wrote her first stories. She had a long and successful career, illustrating and writing many picture books of which 'The Sun Egg' is one of the most popular. She also wrote several collections of fairy tales.

Little Red Riding Hood
The French writer Charles Perrault (1628 – 1703) produced the first collection of fairy tales to include such favourites as 'Cinderella', 'Puss in Boots', 'The Sleeping Beauty' and, of course, 'Little Red Riding Hood'. The story first appeared in *Contes de ma mère l'oye* in 1697. Its great popularity has ensured its inclusion in many later collections.

The Black Bowl
This story was first published in English in 1910 in a collection compiled by Grace James. She collected from many sources, including the *Koji-Ki* or *Record of Ancient Matters*, an ancient Japanese text which was compiled in the eighth century.

The Smith and the Little People
The changeling child is a very common theme in fairy tale, especially in the Celtic realms. The child was usually stolen for its great beauty and kept as a future wife or husband for the fairy queen or king but, as here, the substitution was sometimes made to provide a servant of greater strength and size. I have adapted this version from Barbara Ker Wilson's *Scottish Folk Tales and Legends*.

Strong Wind the Invisible
This Native American version of the Cinderella story comes from *Canadian Wonder Tales* by Cyrus Macmillan, published by John Lane in 1918. The European immigrants brought many of their traditional stories to America where they soon became absorbed into the North American tradition, acquiring a special flavour all of their own en route.

Anansi and the Magic Pot
Anansi or Anancy originally came from Africa before going to the Caribbean where he is known as Brer (or Brother) Anansi. He is one of the best known tricksters in mythology, sometimes appearing as a spider, sometimes as a man. Sir George Dasent included this Anansi story in the second edition of his *Popular Tales From the Norse*, published in 1859. These stories had been related to him by his African nurse as he was growing up in the West Indies.

Barefoot Collections — *an imprint of* Barefoot Books Ltd, PO Box 95, Kingswood, Bristol BS30 5BH. Text copyright © 1999 by Fiona Waters. Illustrations copyright © 1999 by Lisa Berkshire. The moral right of Fiona Waters and Lisa Berkshire to be identified as the author and illustrator of this work has been asserted. ISBN: 1 901223 65 5
First published in Great Britain in 1999 by Barefoot Books Ltd. All rights reserved. No part of this book may be reproduced in any form or by any means, electronic or mechanical, including photocopying, recording, or by any information storage and retrieval system, without permission in writing from the publisher. Graphic design by Judy Linard. Colour separation by Grafiscan, Verona. Printed and bound in Singapore by Tien Wah Press (Pte) Ltd.
British Library Cataloguing-in-Publication Data: a catalogue record for this book is available from the British Library.
1 3 5 7 9 8 6 4 2